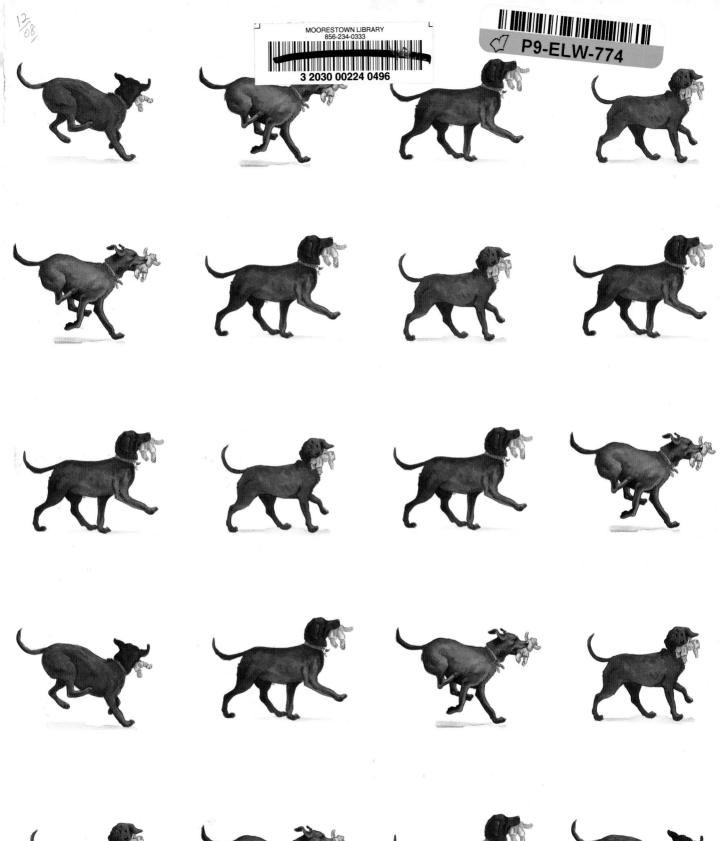

CATIE COPLEY

CATIE COPLEY

written by Deborah Kovacs

illustrated by Jared T. Williams

DAVID R. GODINE • PUBLISHER

BOSTON

For Judy, Jacquie and Ann.   DK

To my parents, to whom I owe it all.
And to Martha and Silas my partners in crime.   JTW

First published in 2007 by
David R. Godine, Publisher
Post Office Box 450
Jaffrey, New Hampshire 03452
www.godine.com

Library of Congress Cataloging-in-Publication Data

Kovacs, Deborah.
  Catie Copley / written by Deborah Kovacs ; illustrated by Jared T. Williams. — 1st ed.
        p. cm.
    Summary: When Catie fails the vision test at Seeing Eye dog school, she is given the unique job of helper at a
big hotel and puts her   special talents to work.
  ISBN-13: 978-1-56792-332-2
  ISBN-10: 1-56792-332-1
1.   Service dogs—Juvenile fiction. [1. Service dogs—Fiction. 2.   Dogs—Fiction. 3. Hotels, motels, etc.—
Fiction.]   I. Williams, Jared   T., ill. II. Title.

  PZ10.3.K8453Cat 2007
  [E]—dc22
                                                                                    2007002435
First Edition
Second Printing, 2008
Printed in China

I believe I was born to do great things.
When I was a puppy, I trained to be a guide dog.
I learned to help blind people get around safely.
This is a very important job.

I couldn't wait to start my new life.
But first, I had to pass a medical test.

The doctor told me some bad news. "Something is wrong with your eyes, Catie," she said. "You don't *see* well enough to be a guide dog."

Impossible! But it was true.

When all the other dogs met their new
people, I had to stay with the trainer.
She hugged me and patted me. She said,
"We will find you another job, Catie.
One that is just right for you."

I am lucky. Soon I got a job at a big, beautiful hotel. Jim takes care of me. He is the concierge. His job is to help all the guests at the hotel. My job is to help Jim.

I stay with Jim's family at night and come to work with him every day. He knows how to scratch me behind the ears—just right. When he puts on his shiny black uniform, he says we look like two peas in a pod.

Everyone is kind to me.
The food is great and my bed is comfy.
At first, the lobby seemed so grand
and so full of hustle and bustle.
There were so many new smells.
I was homesick.
It's hard to make a new start.
But before very long, I came to love my life at the hotel.

Busy days are the best of all.
I take people for walks, visit meetings, and play with children.
I am proud of my job.
Still, I kept hoping to do something really great.
My chance finally came one Saturday morning,

I lay on my bed, smelling sausages. (Sausages are my weakness.)
I heard somebody crying.
It was a little girl.

"I lost Milo," she sobbed.
An old lady patted her on the shoulder.
"There, there," said the old lady.
Jim and I came up close to the girl.

She smelled a bit like sausages, herself.
"What's the matter?" asked Jim.
"Tess has lost her little bear,"
said the old lady.

"My mama gave him to me," said Tess.
"Tess's mama and papa are away on a long trip,"
  said the old lady. "I am Tess's grandma.
  I am taking care of her."
"And now Milo is gone!" Tess sobbed.
"I don't know where he is."
  What does Milo look like?" asked Jim.
"He has little red-striped socks," sniffled Tess.
"He fell into my plate of sausages
  this morning."
"We will do our best to
  find him," said Jim.
  He looked right at me.
  We?
  He wanted me to help!

  I jumped up and wagged my tail.
"Take Catie for a walk while we
  look for Milo," suggested Jim,
  handing my leash to Tess.
  A walk? But…
"Catie knows where to go," said Jim.

I was disappointed.
But it was such a beautiful spring day,
I cheered up fast.
Everyone was in a great mood.

The Duck Tour quacked at us and all the people waved.
Tess and her grandma waved back.
The hot pretzels smelled extra-good.
Even the pigeons seemed friendly.
We strolled down Newbury Street.
Everything and everyone is fashionable there,
especially those yippy little dogs.

At the Public Garden, we walked all the way around the pond.
We watched the ducks swim behind the Swan Boats.
I wanted to jump in to visit them.
But I am too well-behaved.

Tess loved the ducks even more than I do.
But she is not as well-behaved as I am.
She almost fell into the pond. I tugged her back by the shirt just in time.
"Oh, Tess!" said her grandma
When we got back to the hotel, Milo was still missing.

Tess was so sad. She really loved Milo.
Her grandma took her to the Oak Room
for soup and a crusty roll.
They would be leaving soon to take a train home.

"Rest, Catie," said Jim.
Rest? That was the last thing I wanted to do!
I sniffed the air. I wanted to find that bear.
I am supposed to stay near Jim all the time.
But when he got busy with guests, I slipped away.

I went into the Venetian Room, and
looked under every table.
At last, I found an important clue.
It was a little red-striped, Milo-sized sock.
It smelled like sausages.
Milo had been here!
But where was he now?

The banquet staff
had left the back door open.
The scent led me down the corridor.
I snuck downstairs
to the Back of the House.
This is where all the hard work
in the hotel goes on.

I knew Jim would ask everyone in the hotel to look for me. I had to find Milo before they found me. I had to find Milo before Tess left!

I sniffed through the workshop. No Milo.
I sniffed through Private Dining. No Milo.
I sniffed through the kitchen. No Milo.

I went into the Laundry Room.
I saw row after row of rolling carts.
They were loaded with dirty tablecloths,
napkins, sheets, and towels.
I sniffed everywhere.

Finally, I found the smell I was looking for.
With a huge leap, I landed inside a cart.
I pawed through a mountain of tablecloths, sniffing
all the way. And there, right at the bottom, was Milo!

I hurried back up to the lobby.
I knew Jim would be worried.
But I knew he would be proud of me, too.

I had done something important.
I had done something really great!
I was really helping somebody!

I dropped Milo at Jim's feet.
"Catie Copley!" Jim scolded.
I kept my head down and tried to look ashamed.
Jim picked up Milo .
We went to the doorway of the Oak Room.
Jim waved to Tess and held up Milo.

Tess and her grandma rushed up to us.
"Milo!" said Tess.
"Catie found her!" said Jim.
Tess hugged Milo.
Tess hugged me.
"Catie! You are my hero!" she cried.

I looked up at Jim, with a little doggy smile.
He smiled back, shaking his head.
I could tell he wasn't really mad.
He knows I need to help people.
"Ah Catie," he said.
He scratched me behind the ears, just right.
I can't wait for the next adventure!